Gargoyles
Don't Drive
School Buses

There are more books about the Bailey School Kids!
Have you read these adventures?

Gargoyles Don't Drive School Buses

by Debbie Dadey
and
Marcia Thornton Jones

illustrated by John Steven Gurney

A
LITTLE **APPLE**
PAPERBACK

SCHOLASTIC INC.
New York Toronto London Auckland Sydney

ISBN 0-590-99785-8

12 11 10 9 8 7 6 5 4 3 2 1   6 7 8 9/9 0 1/0

Printed in the U.S.A.   40

First Scholastic printing, February 1996

Book design by Laurie Williams

For those who watch over us,
for our many blessings.

— M.T.J. and D.D.

Gargoyles
Don't Drive
School Buses

1

New Driver

Eddie kicked the dirt under the oak tree with his muddy tennis shoe. It was after school, and Eddie, Melody, Liza, and Howie raced to the playground's oak tree as soon as the last bell rang. "I didn't think teachers were allowed to give homework on the weekends," Eddie griped.

Melody twirled her black pigtail. "Mrs. Jeepers can assign what she wants."

Howie and Liza nodded. Nobody dared argue with their third grade teacher. If they did, her flashing green eyes and glowing brooch always took care of it. Most third-graders were convinced Mrs. Jeepers was a vampire so they weren't about to complain to her when she made them do homework. Even if it was Friday.

1

"But I don't know anything about rocks," Eddie complained.

Melody giggled. "You should know lots about rocks, since your head is full of them."

Howie ignored Melody and looked at Eddie. "That's why Mrs. Jeepers wants us to write a report," Howie told his best friend. "We can learn all about rocks at the public library."

"The library!" Eddie yelled. "Are you crazy? I wanted to play soccer all weekend."

"Howie's right," Liza said. "Besides, the library is a neat place to spend the weekend."

Melody nodded. "And if we hurry, the bus driver might give us a ride." The four friends raced across the playground. Eddie zipped ahead of the other kids.

"Watch out!" Melody screamed. She pulled Eddie out of the school driveway just as a big yellow bus drove up.

Eddie pushed Melody's arm away. "Don't worry, Mrs. Gurney would never run over her favorite red-headed kid."

"That's not Mrs. Gurney," Melody said, pointing to the new bus driver. "I've never seen that man before."

"Who is that new bus driver?" Eddie asked. "He looks like a bulldog with a broken heart."

"Eddie!" Liza squealed. "You shouldn't say that about people. Everyone is different in his or her own special way."

"And you are especially different." Eddie snickered.

Howie ignored Eddie's teasing and asked Melody, "What happened to Mrs. Gurney?"

Melody shrugged her shoulders, but Liza spoke up. "My mother said Mrs. Gurney is having surgery."

"Maybe she's having an operation to get nicer," Eddie said.

"Oh, Eddie," Melody sighed. "Surgery is nothing to joke about."

"It's no big deal," Eddie told them. "I had my tonsils taken out."

Liza put her hand to her throat. "Weren't you scared?" she asked. "Didn't it hurt?"

"Maybe a little," Eddie admitted, "but I got to miss school and my grandmother let me eat huge bowls of ice cream. It was great!"

"Speaking of huge," Melody interrupted. "Look at the size of the new bus driver." The four kids stared as a big gray-haired man wearing sunglasses ducked out of the yellow school bus.

"Yikes!" Howie gasped. "I've seen that man before!"

2

Mr. Stone

"Excuse me, sir," Melody said. "Could you give us a ride to the library?"

The new bus driver slowly took off his sunglasses and looked down at Melody and her friends. His gray hair was combed into points behind his ears and his eyes looked like a cloudy sky. Even his droopy wrinkled skin looked gray. The bus driver took a long sad breath and nodded.

Melody, Howie, and Eddie climbed inside the bus and sat down a few rows behind the new driver, but Liza smiled and held out her hand. "Hello, my name is Liza. What's yours?"

The driver slowly reached out to shake Liza's hand. "My name is Mr. Stone," he said in a deep gravelly voice.

Liza's smile faded and she pulled her hand away. "Welcome to Bailey School," she said, but she didn't sound quite as friendly as before.

Mr. Stone nodded as if his neck were stiff. Then he turned away, slowly put on his sunglasses, and started the bus.

Liza made her way down the aisle with a frown on her face, and sat next to Melody. "What's wrong with you?" Eddie asked from the seat behind.

Liza buried her hands in her pockets. "Mr. Stone has the coldest hands," she said.

"It is chilly today," Melody said as the bus roared around a corner.

"This was worse than chilled," Liza said softly. "His hands were stone cold and so hard. It gave me a weird feeling."

Howie's eyes got big. "Mr. Stone gives me a strange feeling, too," he said. "I know I've seen him somewhere before."

"Where?" Eddie asked. "On a most-wanted poster?"

Howie shook his head. "I can't remember, but he looks very familiar."

Just then, the bus groaned to a stop in front of the Bailey City Library and Mr. Stone stiffly turned around to face the four friends.

"The library," he said in his slow raspy voice, "is a favorite spot of mine. It is so . . . homey."

Then he turned away and waited for Melody, Howie, Liza, and Eddie to climb out of his bus. Once they did, the bus creaked away from the curb, leaving the kids standing alone in front of the ancient stone building.

"How could anybody think of this place as homey?" Melody asked.

"I think it's beautiful," Liza said. "Old buildings like this are rare. Especially ones with those fancy gargoyles." Liza

pointed to a row of five concrete monsters staring down at them from the top of the old building.

Howie nearly choked when he looked where Liza pointed. Eddie patted Howie on the back. "Are you all right? You act like you just saw a ghost," Eddie said.

"Close," Howie whispered. "I thought I saw one of the gargoyles move!"

3

The End of the Gargoyles

Eddie laughed so hard he had to sit down on the library steps. "Your brain has turned to concrete if you think stone monsters can move."

"Eddie's right," Melody told Howie. "The setting sun must have blinded you for a minute. Maybe you'll see better if we go inside."

Howie gave the giant gargoyle one final glance before following his friends into the gloomy library. It was even darker than usual because a broken window had been covered with a board. The kids had to sidestep a barrel used to catch drips from a leaky pipe.

"This place is a mess," Melody said.

Howie nodded. "That's why a new library is being built."

"A new library?" Liza asked. "But I like this one."

"This one is about to fall down," Eddie pointed out.

Howie nodded. "The new library will be huge. There's a picture of it by the counter. I'll show you."

Melody, Liza, and Eddie followed Howie to the librarians' counter to look at the sketch. As soon as the librarian saw them, he dropped a pile of books and walked over to the picture. "Isn't the new building simply gorgeous?" Mr. Cooper asked.

Liza shrugged. "All that glass and steel on the new building looks cold. It's not nearly as interesting as this one. I think we already have a gorgeous library."

Mr. Cooper nooded. "Of course we do. But it is a terrible mess. The plaster is cracked and the roof and pipes leak. Why, on a rainy day I have to carry an umbrella just to shelve books."

"Maybe they could patch the roof," Melody suggested.

Mr. Cooper sighed. "That would only solve part of the problem. You see, this library is way too small for our growing collection of books. The new library will be much bigger. And I just can't wait!"

"But what will happen to this building?" Liza asked.

Mr. Cooper shrugged. "I suppose a wrecking ball will tear it down."

With that, Mr. Cooper went back to his stack of books. Liza looked at her friends. "They can't tear down this beautiful building," she said. "It's one of the oldest buildings in Bailey City."

"It's just a drafty old building," Eddie pointed out.

"But it's a beautiful drafty building," Liza argued. "And the only one with gargoyles. A wrecking ball would mean the end of the gargoyles."

15

"I could live without those gargoyles," Melody admitted. "They give me the creeps. It's like they're always staring at me."

"They're not the only things staring at us," Howie whispered.

"What do you mean?" Eddie asked.

Howie motioned to the shadows near the reference shelves. "I don't want to scare you, but I think someone has been watching us."

"Who would spy on a bunch of kids?" Eddie asked.

"I don't know," Howie said slowly. "But I plan to find out."

4

The Roof

"Follow me," Howie said and raced off toward the reference shelves. The four friends skidded to a stop behind a tall case of encyclopedias.

"We just missed him," Eddie said. "He went through there." Eddie pointed to a heavy steel door marked ROOF: DO NOT ENTER.

"Why would anyone go there?" Melody asked.

"To get away from us," Howie said. "But it won't work because we're going to follow him."

"We can't," Liza insisted. "It says DO NOT ENTER."

Eddie shook his head. "It's the only way to find out who was watching us. I'm going . . . "

"You *are* going," Mr. Cooper said, stepping around the encyclopedias. "You're all leaving the library this minute. First, you run through the fiction section and now you're talking loudly."

"We're sorry, Mr. Cooper," Liza apologized.

Howie and Melody nodded. "We promise to be quieter," Howie whispered. "We really need to get some books for school."

Mr. Cooper tapped his foot. "All right, but I'll escort you to the card catalogue personally. I want you kids out of here soon. It is already getting dark outside."

The four kids followed Mr. Cooper without a word. Within thirty minutes they had a stack of books about rocks to choose from. Eddie chose two that had lots of pictures and scooted out of the library to wait for his friends.

Liza and Melody skipped out of the door ahead of Howie. Each of them had books tucked under their elbows.

"I didn't know there was so much to learn about rocks," Melody said. "I always thought a rock was just a rock."

Howie nodded. "Maybe we could split up the work. Each one of us could choose between sedimentary, igneous, and metamorphic rock."

"I don't even know what those are," Liza said.

"I think Howie's right," Melody said. "Eddie, what do you think about splitting up the research?"

"I think we should split, all right," Eddie

whispered. "And I'm not talking about rocks."

"What's wrong with you?" Howie asked.

Eddie looked up at the sky. "Strange things happen when it gets dark."

"I hate it when it starts getting dark so early," Liza agreed.

"Weird things do happen in the dark," Howie said slowly, looking up at the statues on the roof. "Like stone monsters coming to life!"

5

Cold Gray Day

"Do you really think those gargoyles can move?" Liza asked softly. It was the next afternoon and the four kids were gathered in front of the library. It was a chilly day and clouds filled the sky.

Eddie shook his head. "I know those five gargoyles can't move. They're solid rock." Eddie pointed to the statues perched on the roof of the library.

"Didn't you say there were five gargoyles?" Howie asked hoarsely.

"I know there are five," Eddie said. "I counted them last night while I was waiting."

"Well, there are six now," Howie said. "And one of them looks exactly like Mr. Stone!"

"That can't be," Liza said. "Eddie prob-

ably just counted wrong. There are definitely six gargoyles now."

"I don't know how to tell you guys this," Howie said, "but there are legends that say gargoyles can come to life at night."

Eddie snickered. "There are legends around Bailey Elementary that you're crazy," Eddie told Howie.

Liza shivered and shoved her hands in her pockets. "It is pretty strange that the statue looks like Mr. Stone."

"Like a living gargoyle," Howie said.

Melody rolled her eyes. "Are you saying Mr. Stone *is* a gargoyle?"

"Howie, you read too many rock books last night," Eddie told his friend. "Your brain is one brick short of a full load."

"I don't care what you say. I think Mr. Stone was the one watching us yesterday," Howie said.

Liza jumped up and down. "And then he ran up to the roof!"

"Exactly," Howie agreed. "Mr. Stone went up to the roof and later turned into the sixth gargoyle."

"No way!" Melody and Eddie said together.

"It is possible," Liza said softly.

Eddie pulled his baseball cap off and pointed it at Liza. "Gargoyles are just carved rock. They don't come to life."

"And they definitely don't drive school buses," Melody agreed.

"You have to admit he looks a lot like that statue," Liza pointed out.

Eddie shrugged. "So? That doesn't make him a gargoyle."

"But he could be," Liza argued.

"Liza's right," Howie said. "We have to do something."

"And I know exactly what I'm going to do," Eddie snapped. "I'm going to prove that the only rocks around Bailey City are in your heads."

"What are you going to do?" Melody asked.

Eddie pulled his baseball cap down tight over his red curly hair. "Just follow me and I'll prove there are no living gargoyles in Bailey City!"

6

Doomed

The three friends followed Eddie into the library. Only today the big bucket was gone and the building seemed much brighter.

Mr. Cooper and another librarian stood in front of the window that had been boarded up. "It doesn't make any sense," Mr. Cooper said. "Why would anyone go to all that trouble to repair a window in this library?"

The other librarian reached out to touch the colorful stained glass. "This is exactly the way the window looked when I was a kid," she said. "It must have cost a fortune to fix it. Who would do such a thing?"

"Whoever did it must not like leaky pipes, either," Mr. Cooper pointed out,

"because they were fixed during the night, too."

"It's a miracle," the other librarian said.

"It doesn't matter," Mr. Cooper interrupted. "This building must still be replaced. Bailey City needs a bigger library, and that's just what we're going to get."

Liza pulled her friends behind a shelf of books. "Did you hear that? Someone besides me wants to save the library."

"We don't have time to worry about this old building," Eddie told her. "We have a gargoyle to hunt down. Now let's go."

"Where?" Liza, Melody, and Howie asked at once.

"To the gargoyles' perch," Eddie said. "The roof."

"Mr. Cooper would never let us go on the roof," Liza told him.

Eddie glanced at Mr. Cooper just as the librarian eyed the four kids in their huddle. "You're right," Eddie said fast. "I'll take care of Mr. Cooper. You go hunt for gargoyles."

Without waiting for them to answer, Eddie stuck his hands in his pockets and sauntered across the library's lobby, whistling the whole way. Melody, Liza, and Howie saw Mr. Cooper shake his head.

"Young man," Mr. Cooper hissed from across the big room. "Shhh."

But Eddie acted like he hadn't heard a thing. Instead, he walked up to a towering stack of books and pulled one out from the very bottom. The entire pile tumbled to the floor.

"Stop! Stop!" Mr. Cooper raced toward Eddie.

Eddie slapped his own forehead. "Ooops!" he said loud enough for his friends to hear all the way across the library. "I'll pick them up, Mr. Cooper. Don't you worry about a thing."

Eddie bent down to grab a book. But when he did, he bumped into another stack and sent the books toppling to the floor with a loud bang.

"Oh, my," Eddie said in his most innocent voice. "I'm just so clumsy today. I'm sorry. But I'll clean it up. I promise."

Mr. Cooper's face was splotchy red. "Don't bother," he told Eddie. "I'll take care of this."

Eddie slapped Mr. Cooper on the back. "I wouldn't think of it. I made the mess, and I'll help clean it up. Do they go in any sort of order?"

Melody, Liza, and Howie were afraid Mr. Cooper might faint right there in front of them. But he didn't. As Mr. Cooper and Eddie gathered up the books, the three friends quietly sneaked to the back of the library and slipped through the door that said DO NOT ENTER.

7

Missing Gargoyle

"What are we looking for?" Melody asked as they climbed the steps to the roof of the library.

"Shh," Liza warned. "If Mr. Stone is up here, we don't want him to hear us."

"If Mr. Stone is up here, we could be in big trouble," Howie said softly. "There's no telling what a mad gargoyle might do to three scared kids."

"You don't really believe those gargoyles are alive, do you?" Melody asked. "They're just rocks."

Howie stopped climbing the steps and faced Melody. "I do know that legends are full of living gargoyles that fly through the night. Why should Bailey City gargoyles be any different?"

Melody shrugged. "But why would a

gargoyle choose to come to life now?"

"Maybe he's trying to save the library," Liza said softly. "After all, if it's torn down, he'll be destroyed, too."

"That would be terrible," Howie said.

Liza nodded. "That's why we have to prove Mr. Stone is real. And then we have to help him."

"Then let's do it," Howie said as he started climbing the steps again.

The roof of the library was littered with pebbles, and a row of doves cooed from the corner farthest from the giant gargoyles. Howie, Liza, and Melody had to look way up to see the heads of the stone monsters.

"One, two, three, four, five, six," Melody counted. "Six gargoyles. What does that prove?"

"Nothing," Howie said. "Let's look closer at the one on the corner."

The last gargoyle squatted down on two

huge feet with long claws for toenails. Its giant chin rested in its big hands as if caught in the middle of an important thought. But that's not what startled the kids.

"Look at his eyes and cheeks," Liza whispered. "They look exactly like Mr. Stone."

Melody nodded. "Maybe the artist used Mr. Stone as a model."

"Or maybe," Howie said slowly, "it really is Mr. Stone!"

Liza took a step back, but Melody shook her head so hard her pigtails bopped her on the nose. "This is just a statue. See?" With that, Melody slapped the statue as hard as she could on its giant arm. "Now, let's get out of here before Mr. Cooper catches us."

As the three kids turned to leave, Howie grabbed Melody's arm. "What's that?" he asked.

"What?" Melody said.

Howie bent down, reached in the shadows behind the sixth gargoyle, and pulled out a pair of dark sunglasses.

"Who would've left their sunglasses up here?" Liza asked.

"Didn't Mr. Stone have sunglasses like these yesterday?" Howie asked.

Melody shrugged. "A lot of people wear sunglasses when they drive. We'll leave them in the lost and found. We'd better get downstairs before Mr. Cooper throws Eddie out of the library for good."

Mr. Cooper had just placed the last book on the pile when Melody, Liza, and Howie raced across the library lobby.

"Come on, Eddie," Melody said, grabbing his arm before he could send a set of encyclopedias crashing to the floor. "We need to find more books about rocks."

Howie found the section on rocks and pulled several off the shelf. He handed

them to his friends. "Let's check the index in these books to see if they have the information we need."

The three friends piled the books on a nearby table and started skimming through the pages. They could tell by the darkening shadows that it was getting close to dinnertime.

Mr. Cooper looked tired when he spoke to them. "You better find what you need today, because tomorrow we're moving everything out to a warehouse."

"Why?" Liza asked.

Mr. Cooper pointed out a window to a group of men huddled on the sidewalk. "That's the demolition crew. It looks as if they're ready to start the new library. So you'd better scoot."

Liza rushed to the front doors and pressed her nose against the glass. "We have to stop them!" she told her friends.

Eddie didn't seem too worried. "If they turn this place into a pile of rubble, maybe

we won't have to do that report for Mrs. Jeepers."

"Is that all you can think about at a time like this?" Liza said. She forgot to whisper and her voice echoed through the silent library.

Mr. Cooper hurried across the lobby and pushed open the door. "I believe you children need to play somewhere else." Then he gently pushed the four friends outside.

"We'll bring the wrecking ball on Monday," one of the men on the sidewalk was saying. "We'll have this building torn down in a day."

"It's true," Liza wailed. "The library is doomed."

Just then a huge shadow swooped over the small group gathered on the sidewalk.

Eddie, Howie, Liza, and Melody looked up at the sky. "Oh, no!" Howie gasped. "The sixth gargoyle is missing!"

8

Gothic

"I think it flew that way," Melody screeched and ran around to the back of the building. Liza, Howie, and Eddie followed her to the back steps of the library. All they found was a group of seven-year-olds flying a model airplane.

"There's your gargoyle," Eddie snickered, pointing to the tiny brown plane.

Howie shook his head. "I can't believe that's what we saw. After all, it's getting dark and that's when gargoyles come alive."

"Then you'd better watch out because they might fly through that black hole where your brain should be." Eddie laughed.

"How can you joke when they're going to tear down our library?" Liza said sadly.

She looked as if she were about to cry. "I can't believe they're just going to smash it with a wrecking ball."

"I can't, either," a deep, rough voice said from behind them. The four kids jumped to see Mr. Stone staring at the library. "A friend of mine once said, 'A thing of beauty is a joy forever,'" Mr. Stone told them, never taking his eyes off the library.

"It is a pretty building," Liza agreed.

Mr. Stone smiled at Liza. "It's gothic architecture and very rare in this part of the country. Only a barbarian would harm such a structure."

"Unfortunately, there's a bunch of barbarians in Bailey City," Howie said.

"They're not trying to be mean," Melody explained. "They just want a nice library."

"There's got to be something we can do to save it," Liza said.

Eddie shrugged. "We're just kids, we can't stop progress."

Liza looked at Mr. Stone and smiled. "I'm going to start a petition to save the library. That'll make those barbarians slow down a little."

Mr. Stone put a large hand on Liza's shoulder. When he did, Melody noticed a huge purple bruise on his arm.

Mr. Stone looked ready to cry. Instead, he gulped and smiled back at Liza. "That is an excellent idea," he said. "I would be proud to be the first to sign your petition."

Then Mr. Stone's face grew serious and so did his voice. "I would do anything to protect this library," he said, looking up toward the library roof. Liza smiled, but Howie shivered when he looked at Mr. Stone's hard face.

9

Not Nice

"Isn't he nice?" Liza said as Mr. Stone walked into the library.

"*Nice?*" Howie shrieked. "Nice like a rabid dog! Didn't you hear him? He'd do *anything* to save the library."

"So?" Melody asked.

Howie slapped his forehead and looked at his friends. "Don't you know anything? Gargoyles are trapped in stone forever, unless . . ."

"Unless what?" Melody asked, her eyes wide.

"Unless they are forced to break the spell of stone to fight off great danger. So, Mr. Stone is dangerous. And what about the other gargoyles? What if he decides to wake them up and they start a war to protect the library?"

Eddie patted Howie on the back. "Calm down, buddy boy. You've been eating too much junk food lately. That gray-headed man isn't going to start a war and you know it."

Howie looked at Eddie. "If I can prove to you that Mr. Stone is a gargoyle, will you help us save Bailey City?"

"Oh, brother," Eddie said, rolling his eyes. "What's your plan?"

"Gather 'round," Howie said, "and I'll explain." The four friends huddled together and listened. Then Howie, Liza, and Melody headed home to work on their rock reports while Eddie kicked a soccer ball around his front yard.

At exactly seven o'clock the kids met back at the library. It was already getting dark and the lights from inside the building cast eerie shadows around the four friends. A strong breeze sent scraps of newspaper rustling down the deserted sidewalk.

"I don't know why we're doing this," Eddie complained. "I don't believe in gargoyles coming to life."

"I didn't before," Melody said softly, "but now I'm not so sure."

"What are you talking about?" Howie asked.

Melody took a deep breath and explained. "When we were up on the roof, I slapped the sixth gargoyle in the arm."

Liza nodded. "I remember."

"Well," Melody said, "today Mr. Stone had a bruise on his arm in the exact place I slapped the stone gargoyle."

"That's just a coincidence," Eddie said quickly.

"If there aren't living gargoyles then what's that?" Liza squealed as something flew off the roof and dived toward them.

10

Grave Danger

"Yikes!" Eddie screamed and raced into the library. Liza, Melody, and Howie were close on his heels. They didn't stop until they reached the door that said DO NOT ENTER.

"If you don't believe in gargoyles, why did you run?" Liza panted.

"Aw, that wasn't a gargoyle," Eddie said more bravely than he felt. "I bet it was just one of those model airplanes."

"Those kids went home hours ago," Melody argued.

"Well, the wind is strong," Eddie suggested. "Maybe some old shingles blew off the roof."

"Or maybe gargoyles flew off the roof," Liza interrupted. "Howie said the threat of great danger brings the gargoyles to life. A wrecking ball is very dangerous. The gargoyles must have heard those men talking about destroying the library."

"The gargoyles didn't hear anything because they're nothing but big rocks," Eddie argued.

"Then go up on the roof," Howie said. "When you see that the gargoyles are missing, you'll have to believe us."

"I'll believe you, all right," Eddie laughed. "I'll believe you have rocks in your head." Without bothering to check for Mr. Cooper, Eddie threw open the DO NOT ENTER door.

Outside, the wind had picked up speed and made climbing the steps difficult. Eddie's baseball cap flew off his head and Liza's hair whipped around, stinging her cheeks.

"The wind's too strong," Eddie gasped. "We'll never make it to the roof."

"If we do, we'll blow away!" Liza shrieked.

"We have to go up there!" Howie yelled. "It's the only way to prove they're alive!"

The four friends clung to each other as they slowly climbed the steps. Closer and closer they came to the black night sky. Eddie was on the top step when beating wings slapped through the tar-black sky right above their heads.

"Run!" Eddie screamed. "Run for your lives!"

11

Pigeon Poo

"Did you see them?" Howie panted.

The four friends huddled at the bottom of the steps. Eddie breathed deeply, trying to catch his breath. Then he grinned at his friends. "I saw them all right. But they weren't anything but a bunch of scared pigeons."

"Then why did you run?" Melody snapped.

"The last thing I wanted to be was a pigeon roost," Eddie told her. "I think this whole plan is nothing but pigeon poo, and I'm not playing along with it anymore."

"Oh, yes you are, featherbrains," Howie told his friend. "Let's go." One more time the four friends struggled up the steps. Just as they neared the top, the gusts of wind died down to a cold breeze. Melody shivered and Howie zipped up his jacket.

"What will we do if they're there?" Melody whispered to Liza.

Liza patted Melody on the back. "Don't worry. Mr. Stone wouldn't hurt us because he knows we want to help him."

Eddie, reaching the top first, waited for Howie, Liza, and Melody to join him. "There are your gargoyles," Eddie said, pointing to the stone figures guarding the roof. "All six of them."

Howie slowly sneaked up behind the sixth gargoyle. "They may be here," he said slowly. "But they're not the same as before."

"What do you mean?" Melody asked.

"Look closely," Howie said. "His toenails are shorter and there's that big bruise on his arm."

The four kids squinted at the silent statue. "You can't tell that for sure," Eddie argued. "It's too dark. I think it's all your imagination."

With that, Eddie trotted down the steps and back into the library. He didn't stop until he reached the sidewalk directly below the stony glare of the gargoyles on the roof.

Eddie waited until Howie, Liza, and Melody gathered around him. "I gave you your chance," Eddie told Howie. "All you proved was that those are nothing more than statues." Eddie pointed to the roof without bothering to look.

"Maybe you're right," Howie said softly. "But I was so sure."

"I'm sure of one thing!" Liza shouted with her hands on her hips. "I'm not giving up on Mr. Stone. And I'm not giving up on this library."

"But what can you do?" Melody asked her friend.

"I have an idea," Liza told them. "But I'm going to need your help."

12

Save Our Library!

"Save our library!" Liza shouted. It was late Sunday afternoon and Liza carried a banner in front of the library. Her mother, father, grandmother, and a handful of neighbors were with her when Melody, Howie, and Eddie showed up.

Melody carried a big sign that said SAVE OUR ONLY GOTHIC BUILDING. Howie's computer-made sign said HELP OUR GARGOYLES. Eddie had a sheet of notebook paper that said HELP in big red letters.

"Come on," Liza yelled to them. "Let's march! The movers are coming any minute to box up the books. The demolition is tomorrow!"

"What about the petition?" Melody asked.

Liza held up a long piece of paper. It

had dozens of names on it, including Mr. Stone's. "I got everybody on my block to sign," Liza said, "and we can get more later."

Howie nodded. "I put notices on a bunch of doors and called the radio station."

"That's great! I have a feeling we're going to do it!" Liza smiled and then started shouting, "Save our library!"

The entire crowd walked in front of the stone steps and chanted, "Save our library!" Soon more kids showed up and joined the group. "Save our library!" got louder. Finally, a large group of teachers came, including Mrs. Jeepers and Principal Davis. "Save our library!" was heard all over the neighborhood.

"We're going to do it!" Liza beamed.

But Howie wasn't so sure. "Look!" He pointed to a line of moving vans headed their way.

"Oh, no!" Melody shouted. "They're going to throw us out of here."

"It's all over now," Eddie said. Liza looked ready to cry as the vans got closer and closer.

"Sorry, folks," a man yelled from the moving van. "You'll have to clear out of here."

"No, no, we won't go!" Liza shouted. "Save our library!" The whole crowd started shouting again. "Save our library!"

The man in the moving van rolled his

eyes and made a call on his car phone. Within minutes a big black car pulled up beside the moving vans.

"It's the mayor," Howie yelled.

The mayor walked in front of the moving vans and held his hands up for quiet. "Folks," he said with a smile. "A beautiful new library is planned to open in May. Your picketing will only delay the progress."

"Excuse me, sir." Liza stepped up in

front of the mayor. "But we like the old library."

The mayor's face turned red. "Young lady, the old library is in deplorable conditon. The roof leaks!"

"Actually," Mr. Cooper came out of the crowd and spoke, "someone has mysteriously fixed the roof. It's as good as new."

"Well," the mayor sputtered. "The old library is too little. The plans have already been drawn up for a larger space."

"Couldn't the plans be changed?" asked a voice from the crowd. Liza recognized the rough voice as Mr. Stone's. "Couldn't we build onto the old library instead of tearing it down?"

"Hurrah!" cheered the crowd.

"What a great idea," said Howie. "I wish I had thought of it."

"So do I," said the mayor. "I'll get the committee working on it at once." The crowd cheered again as the mayor strode

to his black car. In just a few minutes the vans and the mayor's car were all gone.

Mrs. Jeepers put her hand on Eddie's shoulder and smiled an odd little half smile. "Now that the library is staying open," she said, "I look forward to seeing your rock report tomorrow."

Eddie gulped. "Don't worry. Rocks are my life."

The crowd began to leave as Liza peered up into the sky. The late afternoon sun made her squint, but she was certain there were only five gargoyles on the roof.

13

King of the Gargoyles

Several months later, the kids stared up at the library. The stone walls and steps had been scrubbed clean, and shiny new glass additions sprawled on both sides of the old library. A new sign stood beside the old steps. The base was stone, but the top had gleaming brass letters covered by a sheet of sparkling glass. It read THE NEW AND OLD BAILEY CITY LIBRARY.

Liza smiled and looked up at the six gargoyles. The late afternoon sun made her squint. "I think the gargoyles are happy now."

"Maybe that means they'll stay up there where they belong," Melody said. "I'm glad Mrs. Gurney is back as our bus driver."

"I have to show you something," Howie told them. "I noticed it when they were building the new additions." He moved his friends up to the library steps. "Now, look up and count the gargoyles."

"There are only five," Liza said. "Mr. Stone must have flown away again."

Howie shook his head. "It's like an optical illusion. You can't see the sixth gargoyle from here because it's hidden behind the others. It all depends on where you stand."

Liza stepped back a little. "He's right. The sixth gargoyle is still there."

Melody put her hands on her hips. "You mean they never moved in the first place?"

Howie's face turned red. "I guess I was all wrong about them coming to life."

"And I was right," Eddie bragged. "You can call me the King of the Gargoyles."

Melody and Howie laughed, but Liza didn't say anything. She just gasped. Was it her imagination, or did the sixth gargoyle wink at her?

Debbie Dadey and Marcia Thornton Jones have fun writing stories together. When they both worked at an elementary school in Lexington, Kentucky, Debbie was the school librarian and Marcia was a teacher. During their lunch break in the school cafeteria, they came up with the idea of the Bailey School kids.

Recently Debbie and her family moved to Aurora, Illinois. Marcia and her husband still live in Kentucky where she continues to teach. How do these authors still write together? They talk on the phone and use computers and fax machines!